Let's Have a Story

All the stories in this book
are based on the everyday
experiences of young
children, and originally
appeared in the journal
Child Education.
They have been collected
together here so that they
may be enjoyed by an even
larger number of young
listeners.

Cover illustration by Desmond Clover

Let's Have a Story

Edited by Mary Bingley

Illustrated by Elizabeth Haines

Evans Brothers Limited London

These stories are taken from *Child
Education* published by Evans Brothers
Limited, Montague House, Russell Square,
London, W.C.1.

This collection © Evans Brothers Limited, 1971
First published 1971
Reprinted 1972

Set in 12 on 14 point Intertype
Baskerville and
printed in Great Britain by
Cox & Wyman Ltd., London
Reading and Fakenham

CSD ISBN 0 237 35211 7   PRA 2975
PB ISBN 0 237 35201 X

Contents

CONTENTS

The mouse ran down the clock

Nancy Northcote

Half-way up the stairs on a small landing in Terry's house stood a Grandfather clock. It was taller than Terry's father, and it chimed every hour – one stroke for each hour of time.

Every night when Terry's mother took him up to bed at six o'clock, they climbed the stairs together, and on the landing they always stopped in front of the Grandfather clock, waiting for it to strike. As soon as it began, Terry would count out loud: 'One, two, three, four, five, six!' And then he would say:

> 'Hickory, dickory, dock,
> The mouse ran up the clock.
> The clock struck one, the mouse ran down,
> Hickory, dickory, dock.'

Then he and his mother would go on upstairs.

But one evening when they stopped in front of the clock, it didn't strike six. It wasn't even ticking. It had stopped altogether!

'Dear me!' exclaimed Mother. 'Daddy must have forgotten to wind Grandfather up!' So she stood on tiptoe to reach for the special key that was kept right on top of the Grandfather clock, and then she wound him up.

'Come on, Grandfather,' said Terry. 'One, two, three . . .'

But Grandfather didn't even give the smallest tick.

'Something must have gone wrong with his works,' said Mother. 'I'll ask Daddy to have a look at him when he comes home.'

So Terry had to go to bed that night without saying 'Hickory, dickory, dock'. And as his father didn't have time to look at the clock when he came home, Terry couldn't say the rhyme for the rest of the week. He missed saying it very much.

But when Sunday morning came, Father said, 'Come on, Terry. We'll have a look at Grandfather.' So they climbed upstairs to the landing, where his father took the special key and tried to wind the Grandfather clock up. But it was already wound tight.

Then father said, 'Stand back a bit. I'm going to take the face case off.'

Terry didn't know what the face case was, but he went back two paces and watched while his father lifted the top of the Grandfather clock right off and set it down on the floor, so that only the shiny metal face was left, with all the wheels and works showing behind it.

'Hullo!' said Father, 'What's this?'

He put his hand up to touch a round bundle of rags and fluff and bits and pieces, which was pushed into one side of the works. And out from it popped a little brown mouse! As quick as lightning it ran down the side of the clock, down the stairs, across the hall and then into the kitchen and across Mother's foot!

'Ow!' she squeaked in surprise, and dropped a whole pile of plates which she was carrying – smash, bang, clatter, all over the floor!

Terry and his father came running down the stairs to the kitchen.

'Quick! Catch it!' cried Father.

But they were too late. The mouse squeezed under the kitchen door and was soon lost in the garden.

So after Father had cleared the mouse's nest out of the clock, it started ticking again. And that night, when Terry and his mother stopped on the landing, it chimed six properly. After he had counted six with the clock, Terry said:

> 'Hickory, dickory, dock,
> The mouse ran *down* the clock.
> The clock didn't work till the mouse ran down,
> Hickory dickory, dock!'

'It didn't work till the mouse ran down, did it, Mummy?' he asked.

'You're quite right, Terry,' answered his mother. 'It certainly didn't!'

William Puss's holiday

Laurena Holt

William Puss was a beautiful black and white cat. He had amber coloured eyes and a magnificent set of long whiskers. He lived with the Green family at Number 4, The Woodlands. Mr and Mrs Green and their two children, Susan and John, were going away on holiday to the seaside.

William Puss wasn't going with them. He didn't like the seaside: he didn't like the water; he didn't like the sand; he absolutely hated seaweed. (He had tried to eat some once and had been very sick indeed.)

But William Puss was going to have his own holiday. He was going to stay with the Macdonald family who lived at Number 6.

William Puss liked the Macdonald family.

He liked Mrs Macdonald because she was kind, and she had a nice, soft, comfy lap to sit on. He liked Mr Macdonald because he always stroked him gently and never tried to ruffle his fur the wrong way.

Mr and Mrs Macdonald had two children, Sarah and Timothy. William Puss liked them, too. They played games with him and they were never unkind – and they never tried to pull his tail like the naughty boys who lived at Number 10.

So, as the Green family went off on their holiday, William Puss began his holiday with the Macdonald family. Mrs Macdonald gave William Puss a basket to sleep in. It was made of brown straw and it had a bright red woollen cushion on the bottom to make it warm and cosy. Then she gave him a blue china saucer for his milk, and a lovely yellow bowl for his fish. William Puss was very pleased with all his new things, and he purred and purred to tell Mrs Macdonald how pleased he was.

One fine warm day in the middle of William Puss's holiday, Mr Macdonald came home at lunch time. William Puss was very surprised, because Mr Macdonald never came home at lunch time. He had his lunch at work.

Mr Macdonald had come home specially. He had bought a surprise present for Sarah and Timothy. It was a tent, a bright green tent, and it was just big enough for them to sit inside.

William Puss wasn't sure that he liked the tent. It seemed to him like a huge green monster.

'Come inside our new tent, William,' called Timothy, going inside.

William Puss crouched down on the grass; then he lay on his tummy and started to wriggle his way towards the tent. And all the time he kept miaowing softly to himself. 'Miaow, miaow,' he mewed, 'I don't like that big green monster.'

Just then Sarah came out of the house carrying a tray. It had a plate of sandwiches and two glasses of milk on it, and William Puss's blue china saucer filled to the brim with cream as a special treat.

'We are going to have a picnic, William Puss,' said Sarah. 'And I've brought you a saucer of cream, so you can have a picnic too.'

William Puss crawled nearer to the tent. He didn't want to miss a picnic, especially if there was cream. The flap of the tent was open, and, just as William Puss was going inside, the flap fell down and hit him 'plop' on the nose. He jumped into the air with fright, and then, with one great leap and a loud miaow, he disappeared under the holly bush.

Sarah and Timothy rushed out of the tent to see what had happened. William Puss glared at them from under the holly bush. All they could see was his big amber eyes and the tips of his front paws.

'William Puss doesn't like the tent,' said Mrs Macdonald, coming into the garden. She had seen what had happened from the kitchen window.

'Oh dear,' said Sarah, 'what shall we do?'

'We will leave the tent up for now,' said Mrs Macdonald. 'If William still doesn't like it by bedtime, then we will have to take it down again.'

'Poor William Puss,' said Timothy. 'He was having such a lovely holiday till now.'

Later that afternoon, when Mr Macdonald had gone back to work, Mrs Macdonald took Sarah and Timothy to see their grandmother. They left William Puss in the garden, as he was having great fun playing among the cabbages.

While they were at Grandmother's house there was a big thunderstorm.

'I hope William Puss doesn't get too wet,' said Sarah.

'I hope he isn't frightened by the thunder,' said Timothy – who was rather frightened of thunder himself.

When the thunderstorm started, William Puss was having a lovely game among the cabbages. He didn't see the lightning, but he heard the thunder. Bang, bang, bang! William Puss was very frightened. He tried to hide under the cabbages, but he could still hear it. Bang, bang, bang!

It was too much for William Puss, and before he realized what he was doing he had run straight across the vegetable garden, across the grass and right inside the tent.

He stopped suddenly when he saw where he was. His fur bristled and his whiskers twitched. Then he explored all round the tent very carefully, not forgetting to sniff in every corner. It was just like a tiny house, and there was nothing at all to be frightened of!

Sarah had left her woolly cardigan in the tent. William Puss thought it would make a fine cosy bed. He snuggled into it and tucked his head under one of the sleeves. He couldn't hear the thunder any more, and it was so snug and warm that he fell fast asleep.

When Mrs Macdonald and Sarah and Timothy came home, they found William Puss still fast asleep inside the tent.

'Isn't he a clever cat?' said Mrs Macdonald. 'He must have sheltered from the storm.'

Just then William Puss woke up. He stretched; he'd had such a lovely sleep and was feeling very happy. He purred and purred to tell them how much he liked the tent.

'We can leave the tent up now,' said Timothy. 'William Puss isn't frightened any more.'

William Puss enjoyed the rest of his holiday. He had lots of picnics with Sarah and Timothy in the tent. And when the Green family came home from their holidays, what do you think they brought home with them? A green tent, just like Sarah and Timothy's. William Puss was so pleased. It was like having a holiday all over again!

The useful hole

Carolyn Adlington

At the bottom of David's garden was a hedge. On the other side of the hedge was a path and then the road. David was digging a hole on the garden side of the hedge. He was five, and this was his own piece of garden, so he was digging a 'useful hole'. In went the trowel, pushing, scooping up the earth and tipping it into a pile. In, push, scoop and tip it went. In, push, scoop and tip. It was hard work and it made him hot, so he stopped for a moment to wipe his face with his handkerchief – just like the gardener next door.

'Hullo, David. What are you doing?'

It was the postman leaning against his bicycle and looking over the hedge.

'I'm digging a useful hole,' said David. He wished he could have leaned against his spade like the gardener next door when he stopped to talk to people, but his trowel was not big enough.

'That sounds a good idea,' said the postman. 'I'd give you a hand, but I haven't delivered all my letters yet.'

'Have you any for me?' asked David.

'Sorry. It's not your birthday, is it?'

'No,' said David.

'Never mind,' said the postman. 'I'll look in tomorrow and see how you're getting on with the hole. Goodbye!'

He went on, and David could hear his bicycle scrunching on the gravel path. He went back to his digging. In, push, scoop and tip. In, push, scoop and tip.

'Hullo, David.'

David looked up again. It was the man sweeping the road, and, through a hole in the hedge, David could see the little cart into which he put the dust and leaves and rubbish.

'Hullo,' said David. 'What have you found today?'

'A-a-ah,' replied the road-sweeper. 'Today I found a magic book. The pages are quite empty, but I can have any story I want. If I want a story about lions and tigers, I just hold the book in both hands, close my eyes and say, 'I wish for a story about lions and tigers'. Then I open the book and there it is. When I have read it, I close the book and the pages are empty again.'

'Ooh!' said David, and then they both laughed. David knew that the road-sweeper had not really found a magic book, but this was a game they played. David always asked him what he had found, and he always pretended he had found something magic.

'What are you doing today, David?'

'I'm digging a useful hole!'

'It looks quite deep. I'd give you a hand, but I haven't swept all my roads yet. I'll look in when I come round next week. I expect you'll be down to Australia by then. Goodbye!'

He went back to his work, and David could hear his brush going swish, swish along the side of the road. In, push, scoop and tip. In, push, scoop and tip. Perhaps he really *would* dig through to Australia, he thought. In, push, scoop and tip.

By Friday, the hole was just deep enough to hide David if he curled up in it. It was ready to be useful.

First, David was a soldier. He pushed his wooden spade over the edge, crouched down behind it and pretended to be watching for the enemy. Then he jumped up, ran to the far end of the garden, and ran back to the hole before the enemy could catch him.

Next, he was a pirate. With his spade under his arm as a telescope, he strode round his ship shouting things like, 'Make him walk the plank!'

After lunch, the children from next door came to play Cowboys and Indians with David in his hole, and his mother brought them out a picnic tea. It really was a very useful hole.

That evening, David's father came to look at the hole.

'I have an idea,' he said. 'Why don't we make it into a paddling pool?'

'Oh, yes!' said David.

They began the next morning. First, David's father went out in his car and came back with a bag of cement, a bag of sand and a tin of paint. Then he brought his spade and helped David to make the hole bigger.

'We need something to make a hard bottom for the pool,' he said. 'I know, we'll use the broken bricks that the builders left.'

They filled the wheelbarrow, pushed it to the hole and laid the bricks, one by one, on the bottom. Then David's father put an old piece of pipe into the ground between them.

'What's that for?' asked David.

'That's going to be very useful indeed,' replied his father. 'See if you can guess what it's for before we finish the pool.'

During lunch, David told his mother all that they had done that morning.

'I think I can guess what that bit of lead pipe is for,' she said with a smile. 'And I believe I have an old bath plug which might fit. Would you like it?'

David looked at his father who nodded and said, 'Thank you. Just what we want. This afternoon we must do something to make the pool smooth. You can't paddle on broken bricks.'

'No,' said David, 'and the water wouldn't stay in.'

'Right,' said his father. 'So we must cover them with cement.'

After lunch they went outside again, and on a board beside the pool, they mixed some of the cement with all the sand and a little water. It made a large, grey mound, a bit like a rather gritty cake mixture. Then David's father, with his spade, and David, with his trowel, spread it carefully over the broken bricks. When they had finished, the pool looked like an extra large saucer with a little hole in the middle where the lead pipe went into the ground.

'Now we must leave it to dry,' said Father. They sat on the grass, feeling very tired after their hard work. Suddenly, David shouted, 'I know what the pipe is for! It's for letting the water out!'

'That's it,' said his father. 'We'll put the plug in when we fill the pool, and take it out when we want to empty it. The water will run down the pipe and away into the ground.'

'As easy as emptying the bath,' said David. 'Have we finished now?'

'Not quite. Water wouldn't stay in the pool as it is. It would slowly seep away through the cement, as cement is not water-proof, so we must paint it. We'll do that tomorrow.'

The next morning, David watched while his father painted. Soon the pool was a beautiful, shiny, light blue, David could hardly wait to fill it with water.

'We must leave the paint to dry,' said his father. 'If it's still sunny and warm when I come home from work tomorrow evening, we'll fill it then.'

At school the next day David could think of nothing but the paddling pool. He told the other children about it, and he painted a picture of it in the afternoon. When he got home, he went straight into the garden with his mother.

'The paint is dry,' he said, and then looked anxiously at the sun. 'Do you think it will still be warm when Daddy comes in?'

His mother smiled. 'I think so. It's been a hot day. Come and have your tea and then you will be ready.'

The sun was still shining when Father arrived home, and they all went out to look at the pool.

'Yes, it's dry,' said Father. 'Come and help me with the hose, David.'

They connected one end of the hose to the tap by the gar-age, and pulled the other end across the garden to the pool.

Then Mother put the plug into the pipe, Father turned on the tap, and they all watched the water splash into the empty pool. It filled very slowly. The water crept up the sides until it was nearly at the top. David turned off the tap. The pool was ready.

'Come and put on your bathing suit, David,' said his mother.

David raced into the house, and was out again in a flash in his new red bathing suit. His mother and father watched as he stepped carefully into the pool. He sat down and splashed with his hands. The blue colour underneath shimmered through the water. It really was a wonderful pool. And what a very useful hole it had been!

I Thought I Saw

I thought I saw a goblin
Near a canterbury bell,
But James, he says it's not,
It's just a flower pot.
James can always tell.

I thought I saw a fairy,
Sitting on a yellow rose,
But James says, 'Can't you see,
It's just a bumble bee.'
James, he always knows.

But when James heard wild Indians,
Rustling through the grass one night,
'It's just the wind,' I said,
As he went up to bed
I do hope I was right.

Kathleen Watkins

Jenny's jumble sale

K. Audrey Strube

It was a cold February day, and the rain was pattering against the window.

Jenny was bored. She wanted to sow seeds in her little garden – black cress seeds and shiny red radish seeds. She had the packets in her apron pocket all ready, but Mother said she must wait for a fine, warm day.

'Why don't you tidy the toy cupboard?' Mother suggested. 'Come along, we'll do it together.'

It was when they began sorting everything out that Mother had an idea. 'Jenny,' she said, 'you could have a jumble sale.'

'What's a jumble sale?' asked Jenny.

'You turn out everything you don't need any more – clothes, toys and books – and ask your friends to come and buy,' explained Mother, 'then the money you take goes to a good cause.'

'What's a good cause?' Jenny wanted to know.

'Children who have no mother or father, like the ones in the big house up the road, are a *very* good cause,' said Mother.

Jenny thought it was a wonderful idea to have a jumble

sale, and she spent a happy morning sorting and carrying everything down to the garage where Mother had arranged two garden benches, one on either side, for stalls.

Jenny piled all the toys and books on one of the benches, while Mother arranged clothes on the other.

'What shall we do with these baby clothes?' asked Mother. 'These little cardigans and tiny vests?'

'I know!' cried Jenny. 'They will make lovely clothes for dolls and teddies.'

So Mother wrote a notice which said: 'Warm clothes for Dolly and Teddy – 1p each.'

Next she cut up small squares of paper, and Jenny carefully wrote the prices: '1p, 2p.'

'Now we must let your friends know about the jumble sale,' said Mother, and she helped Jenny to write 12 little notes which said: 'Jumble Sale for a good cause in Jenny's garage at 2.30 on Saturday. Please come and buy'. And they dropped them through the letter boxes of her friends.

What a busy time they had on Saturday morning! Jenny's older brothers, Simon and David, turned out their den underneath the stairs, and Jenny trotted to and fro with armful after armful of books, puzzles and games, a scooter with a wonky wheel, an old white mouse cage, and a pedal car with no steering wheel.

'More white elephants,' laughed Father, busy at his bench, as Jenny dragged the pedal car into the garage.

Jenny looked puzzled, and Father explained about white elephants.

'They are large useless objects,' he said, 'which may be just what someone is looking for.'

'White elephants are *fun*,' laughed Jenny, carrying another load. This time there was a trumpet with half the stops missing, a cricket bat with no handle grip, a croquet mallet with a broken handle, some Red Indian feathers, a pogo-stick, and a rather battered toy cash register.

'Just the thing for your change,' said David, 'if we can get it to work.'

He tinkered with the cash register for a little while, and then, when Jenny pressed down the lever marked 'Sale', a little bell went ping and the drawer shot open.

'I'll be cashier, if you like,' volunteered David. David was very clever at maths and wanted to work in a bank.

'I'll blow a fanfare on the trumpet to open the sale,' said Simon, who was the comedian of the family, 'and I could auction off all the left-overs at the end.' He rapped on Father's bench with the broken croquet mallet, saying, 'Now, ladies and gentlemen, what am I bid for this old tin can on wheels? Five pence, am I bid? Did you say five pence, the lady over there with the pony tail?'

At twenty-five past two, Father hid behind his newspaper in the sitting-room and Mother disappeared into the kitchen.

In the garage, all was ready. David had a boxful of change in his cash register drawer and his finger on the lever ready to ring up the first sale. Simon, wearing the Red Indian feathers, stood by the gate practising his fanfare. Jenny waited importantly behind one of the two stalls, clutching her musical teddy to give her courage. Behind the other stall, carefully propped up against a camp stool, sat Belinda, the life-sized doll, dressed in her new blue and white checked gingham dress and white ankle socks. She looked very solemn and unblinking.

Then Simon's fanfare sounded and the fun began. What a jumble of sounds filled Jenny's garage as all her friends swarmed in and the sale began! And what a busy time Jenny and Belinda had as their customers turned everything over, searching for bargains.

After 20 minutes the stalls were almost bare, and Jenny's friends had gathered at the back of the garage where Simon, standing on an orange box, was beginning to auction off the oddments.

All alone for a moment, Jenny remembered her musical teddy, and put her hand down to the leg of the bench where she had propped him. He wasn't there! She looked everywhere: between the deck-chairs stacked in a corner, among the old paint pots and brushes on Father's work bench, and in a bin which was used for chicken food. Jenny was in despair. She asked Belinda, the life-sized doll, and she peered anxiously into the doll's clothes box. No teddy. Where could he be?

At that moment, she heard Simon's voice from the back of the garage.

'One teddy, rather bald but still quite cuddly. Does he growl? Now let's see.' He pressed Teddy's tummy and Teddy jingled rather sadly. 'Ah! There you are, madam, one musical teddy. What am I bid? Four pence? Any advance on four pence? Four pence for this very nice musical teddy! Going – going –'

'Stop!' cried Jenny, pushing her way through the crowd of children standing round the auctioneer. 'That's my teddy and he's not for sale!'

'One teddy, going – going – gone, to the lady in the pink cardigan with the cross look on her face,' laughed Simon, thumping his mallet on the garage wall; and jumping down off the box, he lowered the teddy into Jenny's outstretched arms.

'Sorry, Jenny,' he grinned, 'but these things do happen, you know, even in the best planned jumble sales,' and he winked at David.

Just then, Mother arrived with a tray of home-made biscuits and mugs of steaming cocoa for the children. Father wandered in and asked if anyone had change for a fifty pence piece. David emptied the till and quickly counted out 47 pence. 'Near enough,' said Father, pocketing it and handing Jenny a brand new fifty pence piece instead.

The next day, Mother helped Jenny write a letter to the lady who looked after the children at the big house.

'This money,' the letter explained, 'is to buy a toy for one of your children. I am very lucky and have a life-size doll called Belinda with two sets of clothes, one for winter and one for summer. I have a teddy too. He is rather old now, and his fur is a bit patchy, but I love him very much and he plays a tune in his tummy. Perhaps one of your children would like a teddy like mine. Love Jenny.'

The three baby horses

Pat Devenport

In a field on the slope of a hill there were three baby horses. One was dapple grey, one was brown and one was black, and each was just like his mother. Their mothers were very proud of them.

'See what a shining coat mine has,' said the mother of the dapple grey baby horse. 'It is just like water under a leafy tree.'

'See what a shining coat mine has,' said the mother of the brown baby horse. 'It is just like a new chestnut.'

'See what a shining coat mine has,' said the mother of the black baby horse. 'It is just like a ripe blackberry.'

And the three mothers arched their necks and looked very proud indeed.

At first the three baby horses kept very close to their mothers, but soon, as they grew stronger and felt the sun warm on their backs and saw the smoothness of the green grass, they began to play.

Hrish! Up went the heels of the dapple grey baby horse and away he galloped, pr-rumph, pr-rumph, pr-rumph!

Hrish! Up went the heels of the brown baby horse and away he galloped, pr-rumph, pr-rumph, pr-rumph!

Hrish! Up went the heels of the black baby horse and away he galloped, pr-rumph, pr-rumph, pr-rumph!

'Hehehehehehe,' whinnied the dapple grey baby horse, and it sounded just as if he were laughing.

'Hehehehehehe,' whinnied the brown baby horse, and it sounded just as if he were laughing.

'Hehehehehehe,' whinnied the black baby horse, and it sounded just as if he were laughing.

Then they all rolled on the grass, with their long legs waving in the air, and stretched out their necks. For a little while they lay looking at one another, but they didn't lie still for long.

First the dapple grey baby horse stood up and shook himself.

'Prrh,' he blew down his nostrils, and, turning his muzzle into the warm wind, twitched his ears.

Then he trotted to the hedge – umph umph umph umph.

Then the brown baby horse stood up and shook himself.

'Prrh,' he blew down his nostrils, and, turning his muzzle into the warm wind, twitched his ears.

Then he trotted to the hedge – umph umph umph umph.

Then the black baby horse stood up and shook himself.

'Prrh,' he blew down his nostrils, and, turning his muzzle into the warm wind, twitched his ears.

Then he trotted to the hedge – umph umph umph umph.

They all looked over the hedge.

There, across the next field, down the slope of the hill, was the farm. The windows were open to the sun and the curtains were blowing in the wind.

And in the field – well, there was quite a lot.

'Hehehehehe,' whinnied the dapple grey baby horse. 'Hens!'

'Hehehehehe,' whinnied the brown baby horse. 'Sheep!'

'Hehehehehe,' whinnied the black baby horse. 'Ducks!'

They looked at one another.

The dapple grey baby horse pushed gently against the hedge.

The brown baby horse pushed gently against the hedge.

The black baby horse pushed gently against the hedge, and then he pushed a bit harder. Crack, crash, crack, and he was through. It wasn't long before the brown baby horse and the dapple grey baby horse were through the gap he had made, and there they all were in the next field.

They felt that they were perhaps being a little bit naughty, and should not be there at all where their mothers couldn't see them, but . . .

Hrish! Up went the heels of the dapple grey baby horse and away he galloped, pr-rumph, pr-rump, pr-rumph.

Hrish! Up went the heels of the brown baby horse and away he galloped, pr-rumph, pr-rumph, pr-rumph.

Hrish! Up went the heels of the black baby horse and away he galloped, pr-rumph, pr-rumph, pr-rumph.

Over the field they went, chasing the sheep and the ducks and the hens and the turkeys. And, oh dear, what a commotion there was, with everything flying or running all over the field in a great fright – except for those three baby horses who were enjoying it all! And what a noise there was too!

'Baa baa. Maa. Quack quack. Gobble gobble gobble. Cluck cluck. Baa. Qu-a-ck. Quark! Maa. Baa.'

And then the dapple grey baby horse suddenly stood still.

The brown baby horse suddenly stood still.

The black baby horse suddenly stood still.

Over the hill at the top of the field something was coming – and it had a very loud, deep voice; it crawled along the ground and it looked very, very big to the three naughty baby horses.

'D-d-d-d-d-d-d-d,' it stuttered and growled as it came. 'D-d-d-d-d-d-d-d.'

'Hehehehehehe,' whinnied the dapple grey baby horse, and it didn't sound as if he were laughing this time, for he was far too frightened. 'It must be a dragon.'

Off he galloped for the hole in the hedge, pr-rumph, pr-rumph, pr-rumph.

Off the brown baby horse galloped for the hole in the hedge, pr-rumph, pr-rumph, pr-rumph.

Off the black baby horse galloped for the hole in the hedge, pr-rumph, pr-rumph, pr-rumph.

And, oh dear! They couldn't find it! They galloped up beside the hedge and down beside the hedge, and all the time they could hear 'd-d-d-d-d' behind them and could smell the smoke which was coming out of the dragon's mouth. It wasn't such fun to be chased themselves, they thought, especially by such a dreadful thing as a dragon.

Then they found the gap and, as they crashed through it, there were their dear mothers trotting towards them to find out what was the matter.

'Hehehehehehe,' whinnied the dapple grey baby horse, pressing close to his mother's side. 'There's a dragon.'

'Hehehehehehe,' whinnied the brown baby horse, pressing close to his mother's side.

'We won't chase the sheep again.'

'Hehehehehehe,' whinnied the black baby horse, pressing close to his mother's side. 'Nor the hens, if only the dragon will go.'

The three mothers looked over the hedge and then they looked at one another.

'P—rrrh.' They blew down their nostrils so that they shouldn't smile. 'You silly little horses. That's not a dragon. It's only the farmer on a tractor.'

But whether it was a dragon or a tractor didn't matter very much. The baby horses would *never* chase the sheep and hens again!

Cindy

Barbara Ashley

Cindy was a little black kitten. She was as black as a piece of coal. When she was happy she made a noise like this, 'Purr, purr, purr.'

Cindy belonged to Sylvia, who was four years old. Each morning when Sylvia got up she helped her mother to give Cindy a saucer of milk. One morning Mother let her pour the milk out of the big jug into Cindy's saucer all by herself. This made her feel so happy that she went 'Purr, purr, purr,' just like Cindy. Mother laughed and said that Sylvia had better have some milk as well, although one kitten in the house was really quite enough!

After breakfast, Sylvia and Cindy played with a ball. Sylvia threw it down the hall and Cindy went scampering after it. She knocked it against the wall with her paws and jumped in surprised when it bounced back and hit her on the nose.

Just then there was a ring at the door, and Mother went to answer it. It was the baker. His name was Bill and he was a great friend of Sylvia's.

'May I carry the loaf into the kitchen?' asked Sylvia. 'Of course you can,' said Mother, asking the baker for a large white loaf.

Sylvia took the loaf from Bill and carried it carefully into the kitchen, where she put it on the table. Mother paid for the bread, and Sylvia heard her saying goodbye to Bill and shutting the door.

'Where's Cindy?' asked Mother, as she came into the kitchen. 'In the hall,' said Sylvia, and she skipped out of the room calling 'Cindy, Cindy,' at the top of her voice.

Cindy was nowhere to be seen. Sylvia looked under the stairs, but she wasn't there. She couldn't be in the dining room because the door was shut, so Sylvia ran upstairs and looked in the front bedroom and the bathroom, but she wasn't there either. Then she looked in the back bedroom, but she still couldn't find her. So she ran downstairs shouting, 'Mummy, Mummy, Cindy's lost. I can't find her anywhere.'

'I know,' said Mother. 'She must have run out when I opened the door to Bill, the baker. We'll go out and look in the garden.'

So Sylvia and her mother went into the garden and called and called, but there was no sign of the little black kitten. They looked in the front garden and then went round the back. Sylvia looked under all the bushes and in Father's wheelbarrow, and in all the other places she thought a little kitten might hide. Then Mother had to go in to get the dinner ready. 'Don't worry,' she said. 'Cindy will come back when she's hungry.'

Sylvia stayed in the garden, feeling very sad. Suddenly she heard Mother calling, 'Sylvia, Sylvia, come here quickly.' Sylvia ran up to the house and saw Mother standing by the coal shed. 'Look,' she said.

Sylvia looked into the coal shed and gasped. 'Mummy, what is it? I can see two lights coming at me.'

'They're Cindy's eyes,' said Mother. 'She's so black that you can only see her green eyes shining in the dark.'

Mother reached in and lifted out the naughty little kitten. 'She must have squeezed in through that crack in the door,' she said. 'We must ask Daddy to nail a piece of wood across it when he comes home from work.'

Sylvia hugged Cindy. 'You are very naughty, Cindy,' she said, 'but we are so glad to see you that we can't be cross.'

When Father came home from work, Sylvia told him all about Cindy's adventure. He laughed and said he would put a piece of wood across the crack in the coal house door when he had had his tea. Then at least they would be sure that next time Cindy got lost she wasn't in with the coal!

Richard's little house

Karen Jones

Richard's birthday was on a Monday. He was four years old, and he had some fine presents. There was a shiny red tricycle from Mother and Father, a clockwork train from Granny and Grandpa, and a little blue boat to play with in the bath, from his friend Susie, who lived next door. But there was no present from Uncle John – just a birthday card with a message inside: 'I will bring your present with me when I come to lunch on Saturday. Love from Uncle John.'

All that week Richard was very busy. When it was fine and sunny he played in the garden on his new tricycle, and when it was wet he played indoors with his new train. But he kept on wishing that Saturday would come, and wondering what Uncle John's present could be.

At last it was Saturday. As soon as Richard had finished his breakfast he ran to the sitting room window to watch for Uncle John's little grey car.

'He won't be here for quite a while yet, Richard,' laughed Mother. 'Remember that he has to drive all the way from London.'

'Oh, I do wish he would hurry up,' said Richard. 'I want to see what my present is.'

'The time will go much more quickly if you go and play in the garden instead of sitting by the window doing nothing,' Mother said.

So Richard went into the garden and rode round on his tricycle: he pretended that he was the milkman, leaving his bottles of milk on the doorsteps of all the houses. He was having such fun, and had quite forgotten about Uncle John, when suddenly he heard a car draw up outside. He ran round to the front of the house, and was just in time to meet his uncle coming up the path.

'Hallo, Richard,' said Uncle John. 'I'm sorry your birthday present didn't arrive on the right day, but I thought I'd better bring it down myself, so that I could show you what to do with it.'

'Oh, please, can I see it now?' asked Richard.

'Oh, let Uncle sit down and have a cup of coffee first,' said Mother.

'No, thank you,' Uncle John said. 'It will take us a while, so we'll start right away. This is your present, Richard. I wonder if you can guess what it is.'

Richard was very surprised when he saw the present. It wasn't wrapped in lots of brown paper and string, like his tricycle had been when it came, and it wasn't a brightly coloured parcel like the other presents. It was a big, green canvas bag, about as big as his mother's shopping basket, with something very heavy inside it.

'Let's take it into the back garden,' said Uncle John, 'then we'll unpack it and you'll be able to see what it is.'

So they took the mysterious bag on to the lawn, and Uncle John helped Richard to open it.

When they had emptied everything out, Richard was more puzzled than ever. There were four pieces of wood, lots more green canvas, all neatly folded up, and a paper bag full of little metal rods, each with a hook at the end. Richard just stood and stared at the strange things; he'd never seen a present like this before.

'Now,' said Uncle John. 'I'll show you what to do next.'

He took two pieces of wood and fitted them together to make a long pole, a little taller than Richard.

'You hold this,' he said, 'and mind you hold it upright!'

So Richard stood holding the pole, wondering whatever was going on, while Uncle John unwrapped the green material and shook it out. Then he fixed the canvas over the top of Richard's pole and began to put the hooks through some loops in the edge and push them into the ground.

'Now do you see what it's going to be?' he asked.

'It's a tent!' cried Richard. 'A real little tent of my very own. Oh, Uncle John, it's lovely!'

'Wait a bit,' said Uncle John, smiling. 'We haven't finished yet. Now you must take this other pole and hold it while I put in the rest of the pegs.'

Soon they had finished putting up the tent, and there it stood on the lawn, just like a little house.

Richard went into it very carefully, so as not to knock the poles over. He was so pleased that he didn't know what to say. It looked beautifully green and cool inside. Richard could just stand up in it, but Uncle John had to go down on all fours to get in.

'Well, Richard,' he said, 'do you like your present? When you're bigger you'll be able to go camping. You can see it's big enough to lie down and sleep in.'

'And I can pretend it's my house, and park my tricycle outside the door,' said Richard, 'and Susie can bring her dolls and her tea set and we can play mothers and fathers.'

Just then Richard's father came home for lunch.

'Oh, Richard, what have you got?' he said.

'It's a tent, Daddy. Uncle John's given me a tent of my very own.'

'Well you are a lucky boy,' said Father. 'Wait a minute, I think I've got something in the shed that might be useful to you.'

He disappeared into the garden shed, and a minute later he came out again carrying a large piece of rubber sheeting and a small wooden stool.

'You could use this as a groundsheet, so that you don't get wet or muddy if the grass is damp,' he said, 'and you can have the stool to sit on, or else you can sit on the ground and use it as a table.'

Uncle John helped Richard's father to spread the ground-sheet over the grass inside the tent. It was a tight squeeze for the two big men to get into it – and to put the stool inside.

'Tell Mummy to come and see,' said Uncle John.

So Richard ran into the kitchen.

'Do come and see, Mummy,' he said, 'I've got a real little house with a roof and floor, and a seat to sit on!'

'Good gracious, there couldn't possibly have been a house inside that bag. It was no bigger than my shopping basket,' said Mother, looking very surprised.

'Ah, but it's a special sort of house which folds up very small. Do come and look at it.'

So Mother went out into the garden.

'A tent!' she exclaimed. 'Oh Richard aren't you lucky! I think it's quite the nicest present you've ever had.'

Apricot Sun

At Hastings when we stay up late
To watch the sun dip in the sea,
Says little friend Miranda Kate,
'It looks just like a peach to me.'
But then I say, 'Of course it's not,
It's more like half an apricot.'
We always seem to disagree.

Kathleen Watkins

Jane goes home

Esmé Dain

'My grandpa is meeting me from school today,' Jane said to Mrs Terry, her teacher at the Nursery School, when she arrived one morning.

'My grandpa is meeting me from school today,' she told the children, when she was hanging upside down on the climbing frame.

At twelve o'clock she told the dinner lady, the teacher in the next class and the man who came to repair the roof: 'My grandpa is coming to meet me from school today!'

But when it was time to go home, Grandpa did not come.

Jane and Mrs Terry looked out of the window and saw Jane's Aunt Polly running down the street. She had to run because her large boxer dog, George, was pulling her along on his lead.

'Hello, Mrs Terry,' said Aunt Polly when she reached the door, 'Grandpa's chickens have got out, so I've come for Jane.'

Then she accidentally let go of George, who bounded into the playroom, skidded on the linoleum, and started leaping about and growling at the rocking-horse.

While they were trying to catch him, Uncle Fred arrived with his wife, Aunt Mabel. Uncle Fred was a decorator, and in the pockets of his overalls were two paint brushes and a folding ruler. Aunt Mabel had a bad cold.

'Hello, Mrs Terry,' said Uncle Fred. 'Grandpa's chickens have got out, so we've come for Jane.' Jane thought Uncle Fred smelled beautifully of putty.

'Aatishoo!' sneezed Aunt Mabel.

Then the back door opened and in marched a policeman. This was Jane's Uncle Mac.

'Hello, Mrs Terry,' he said. 'Grandpa's chickens have got out. I hear you have a lost girl here.'

Jane giggled. 'Ooh, Uncle Mac, you are only teasing. I'm not lost at all.'

'Oh, aren't you?' said Uncle Mac, pretending to be surprised. 'I shall have to put that in my notebook.'

By now the passage seemed full of people – and George, who was barking loudly at a golliwog.

Mrs Terry looked a little anxious.

'You haven't any more aunts and uncles, have you Jane?' she asked.

'Oh yes, lots and lots more,' said Jane, 'There's Aunt Harriet, and Uncle David who is a footballer, and Uncle Herbert who takes the children home from the big school in his minibus. But look! Here comes Grandpa!'

And sure enough, there was Grandpa in his Wellington boots, waving his stick and carrying in his pocket an apple for Jane.

'Hello, Mrs Terry,' he said. 'I'm sorry I'm late. You will never guess what happened.'

Grandpa took Jane's hand and everyone was ready to go.

Then it started to rain. It rained so hard that no one could possibly go out in it.

As they waited, Jane counted all the people who had come to fetch her: 'One, two, three, four, five.' Then round the corner swished Uncle Herbert in his minibus. He had taken all the children home from school, and he thought he would give Jane a lift too.

'You'd all better jump in,' he called.

So Jane, Aunt Polly, Uncle Fred, Aunt Mabel, Uncle Mac, Grandpa – and George – hurried into the minibus.

'I've got six people to take me home now,' laughed Jane.

'No seven,' called Mrs Terry, 'I'll have a lift too, if I may.'

'With the greatest of pleasure, Mrs Terry,' said Uncle Herbert. 'The more the merrier.'

So Mrs Terry got in and sat next to Grandpa, who told her all about his chickens getting out, which, of course, was the reason why he had been late fetching Jane from Nursery School!

Jenny and John's circus

Mary Walker

Jenny and John were twins, and their granny and grandad took them to a circus as a special treat.

They had never seen a circus before and thought it was wonderful – the blazing lights, the booming of the band, the smell of sawdust and animals, and the feeling of excitement of the crowd sitting inside the big tent.

Jenny liked the girls in pink frilly skirts riding on brown and white ponies, and the seals who balanced big coloured balls on their noses, but most of all she liked the little dogs, who could run up and down ladders and slide down chutes and even swing themselves on tiny swings.

John liked the lions best of all and thought how grand it would be to be a lion-tamer when he grew up, alone in the cage with the great animals obeying the sound of his voice and the cracking whip. He also liked the clowns who fell about all over the place, getting soaked with water and covered with bags of flour.

When they got home, the twins chattered about the circus, hardly stopping to take a breath between telling Mother and Father about the exciting things they'd seen.

Next morning, when they woke up, they decided to have

a circus of their very own. After breakfast they borrowed an old blanket from Mother to make the circus ring, and folded it till it was almost a circle. Then they collected some old bricks from the end of the garden to put round the edge of the blanket, and borrowed stools and garden chairs for the audience to sit on.

Next they went to find their friends – Sally and Jane from next door, and Peter and Tony from across the road. They all thought it a fine idea to make a circus; Peter and Tony brought their two pet mice and some coloured balls, and Sally and Jane brought their frilly skirts.

Jenny and John called to their dog, Joey, and after a lot of chattering and laughing, a programme was arranged, with all the children who were not in the ring as the audience. John wanted to be ringmaster and announce the different acts, and to his delight Mother came out with a top hat which she'd made from stiff black paper.

'There's a tray of cold drinks and biscuits all ready, so half-way through you can have an interval and refreshments,' said Mother. This was marvellous, and Mother and the rest of the children settled down around the ring while John, proudly wearing the top hat, announced the first act.

'Ladies and gentlemen,' he called in his loudest voice, 'our first act today is the appearance of the two savage white mice, the fiercest in the world, shown by their owners, Peter and Tony.'

Everyone clapped, and Peter and Tony brought their mouse cage into the ring. The mice were delighted to be let out. They cheerfully scrambled up and down the boys' arms and ran about the ring in all directions, while Peter and Tony pretended that they were wild and savage creatures. At last they got them back into their cage, and were applauded out of the ring.

John then announced, 'Ladies and gentlemen, we now show you two of the finest bareback riders ever seen – Sally and Jane!'

Sally and Jane, in their frilly skirts, pretended to trot round the ring on little ponies, doing difficult balancing acts just as though the ponies were really there.

Then, after they had been clapped, John called out, 'And the last act before the interval will be the famous ball balancers, Peter and Tony.'

More applause and back came Peter and Tony, this time with their big coloured balls. They balanced them on their heads, tossed them backwards to each other, and finally laid down and balanced the balls on their feet, which was a great success.

Mother said, 'Now let's have those refreshments,' and she brought out the tray. Even the mice had a crumb each, and there was a whole biscuit for Joey, whose turn it was next.

When everyone had finished, John returned to the ring and announced Jenny and her famous performing dog, Joey. Jenny got Joey to do all the tricks that Mother had taught him – to beg for a biscuit, to pretend to lie down asleep, and to walk on his back legs. Finally, Jenny ran round the ring one way holding a stick for Joey – who was running round the other way – to jump over, and he gave a very good performance.

John's next announcement was that Sally and Jane would give a skipping demonstration, which they did well, for they practised a lot and could do many difficult steps.

When they had been applauded, John cried, 'Our last act, ladies and gentlemen, is the human pyramid, never seen before in any other circus.'

Mother looked a bit surprised as all the children ran into the ring. The three boys knelt down on hands and knees; Sally and Jane climbed gingerly on to their backs, and finally Jenny appeared behind them, standing on a chair, so that it looked as though she was standing on top of Sally and Jane.

Mother clapped very hard and, as the human pyramid collapsed in a giggling heap on the grass, said that such a good act deserved a reward. So when Father came home for dinner he found the greatest circus on earth sitting eating ice-creams in the garden. When he heard about the performance, he asked for a special show to be put on after tea for himself and Granny and Grandad, and so after tea the children did it all again. Everyone agreed that it was just as much fun as the real circus!

Susan and the white cotton

Esmé Dain

Susan was six. She lived in a house with a blue gate. Her granny lived nearby, a little further down the lane, in a bungalow.

One Saturday morning, Susan's mother lost her white cotton. She was sitting in the garden on a pile of cushions doing the mending. Father was cutting the grass and Susan was looking for ladybirds.

'Oh, dear!' said Mother 'Wherever's my white cotton? I must sew a button on Daddy's best shirt.'

They all searched for the cotton. They tipped the sewing basket out on the lawn, and they found a toffee and an earring, but no one could see the white cotton.

'Never mind,' said Mother. 'Perhaps Granny will lend me hers, if Susan will go and ask her.'

So Susan ran down the lane to her granny's.

'Dear, dear,' said Granny. 'I think I used all my white cotton when I made my new curtains. Let's see.'

Granny looked in her box. There was black, blue, green, yellow and a gay orange, but no white cotton at all.

'I thought as much,' said Granny. 'Tell Mummy I'm sorry.'

Then Granny gave Susan a lemon pie with meringue on top to take home for lunch.

'Can you carry it?' she said.

Susan liked lemon pie, so she said she could. Then she kissed her granny and set off, carrying the pie carefully in two hands.

Mr Green lived next to Granny, and he was cutting red cabbages in his garden.

'Here's a red cabbage for your mummy,' he called, 'Can you carry it?'

Susan liked red cabbages too, so she said, 'I've got this lemon pie, but I can carry it, thank you.'

Mr Green put the red cabbage in a carrier bag and hung it over Susan's arm.

Susan had only walked a little way, when she met her friend Jonathan. Jonathan gave Susan a present. It was a ladybird on a leaf in a matchbox.

'Can you carry it?' said Jonathan.

Susan liked ladybirds, so she said, 'I've got this lemon pie and this cabbage, but I'll put the ladybird in my pocket. It's lovely – and I shall call it Fred.'

Mrs Wade lived in the next house. She saw Susan and waved from her window.

Susan put the lemon pie on the wall to rest her arms. Mrs Wade came out carrying a beautiful pale green hat with curly pink feathers. It was for Susan's mother to borrow to wear at a wedding.

'Can you carry it?' asked Mrs Wade.

Susan knew that Mother liked hats, so she said, 'I've got

this lemon pie and this red cabbage and a ladybird called Fred, but I'll try.'

'You'd better carry it on your head, then,' smiled Mrs Wade.

And that's what Susan did.

By now Susan had such a load that she hoped she would not meet anyone else. The lemon pie and the red cabbage were heavy, and the hat was slipping over her eyes. Her face was red and she thought Fred might be unhappy in her dark pocket.

But she could see her blue gate and Father working in the garden. She staggered through the gate.

'Good heavens!' said Father, when he saw Susan, 'Whatever have you got?'

'I thought you'd gone for the white cotton,' said Mother.

'Granny's used it all,' puffed Susan, and she told them all about it.

Mother and Father sat on the grass and admired all the things Susan had brought home. They said Fred was a splendid name for a ladybird.

But Mother looked rather disappointed, because she really wished she had some white cotton.

Father liked to make people laugh. He put on the wedding hat and carried the red cabbage like a bride's bouquet. He marched round singing, 'Here comes the bride.'

Mother laughed so much that she fell off the cushions. And when the cushions rolled away, out fell the white cotton!

'Look what I've found!' shouted Susan.

'Well, I never,' smiled Mother.

And so she was able to sew the buttons on Father's best shirt after all, while Susan watched Fred walk about on the grass.

Summer Breeze

When summer comes,
I like to lie
Among the grass,
And watch the sky.

Often I hear
A little breeze,
Whispering through
The apple trees.

I like it when
It makes me glad,
But yesterday
It made me sad.
I don't know why.

Kathleen Watkins

Debbie's rainy day

Mary Walker

Debbie's birthday was in March, and when she was four her granny's present to her was delivered by the parcel postman in his bright red van. It was a very large parcel, with a lot of string and sticky tape round it. But at last Debbie, who was sitting on the floor surrounded by brown paper and string, had a big grey cardboard box on her lap.

Carefully, she lifted off the lid. Inside was more paper – tissue paper this time, and, as she pulled it out, she could see something underneath, something shiny and blue and white.

'Come on,' said Mother, 'do unfold it. I'm longing to know what can it be.'

Debbie lifted out the bundle – and what do you think it was? A white plastic macintosh, covered with little blue flowers. Debbie was delighted, for her old mac was just a plain red one, and very short and shabby now. There was something else in the box, so Debbie fished about among more tissue paper and found a little hat, made of the same material as the macintosh.

'Oh Mummy!' she said excitedly, 'aren't they lovely? Can I try them on now?'

'Of course you can,' said Mother, 'just let's pick up some

of the paper and string first, then we'll have room to move.'

So Debbie tidied the floor, and, as she lifted up the big cardboard box, she felt that it was still quite heavy. So she put it down again and there, under a last layer of tissue was a pair of white Wellington boots.

'Well,' said Mother, 'you *will* be smart. How very kind of Granny to think of such a lovely present.'

'She must have known they were just what I wanted,' said Debbie, as she put the box, now quite empty, into the kitchen.

Then she took off her slippers and put on the white Wellingtons; they fitted beautifully and looked very smart. Next she put on the macintosh and did up all the silver buttons. Finally Mother put the hat on for her, tucking her pony-tail of hair down inside the collar.

'You do look nice,' smiled Mother, 'go up into my bedroom and see yourself in the long mirror.'

So Debbie clumped up the stairs in her new white Wellingtons, and stood in front of Mother's mirror, turning herself from side to side so that she could see as much as possible of the pretty macintosh and hat.

When she came down again, she said, 'Can we go to the shops now, Mummy, so I can wear my new things?'

'Well, not really, dear,' said Mother, 'you must wait for a rainy day to wear them, because that is what Granny sent them for. Take them off for now and we'll put them in your cupboard. It's sure to rain very soon, and then you can get them as wet as you like.'

So they put the macintosh on a coathanger, and hung the

hat by its loop of ribbon from the hanger too. Then they put them both upstairs in Debbie's cupboard, with the Wellingtons as well.

Of course, when Father came home from work that evening, Debbie had to put them all on again, and he said she looked very smart indeed.

The very next morning Debbie was up early, looking out of her window to see if it was raining – but no, all the paths were dry. All day she hoped for rain, but none came that day, or the next, or the next, and soon March was nearly over.

'I can't understand it,' said Mother, 'we usually have so much rain that I can't get my washing dry, and now everywhere is as dry as a bone.'

'Never mind,' said Father to Debbie, 'April will surely bring rain. You know the old saying. "April showers bring May flowers", so you'll be able to wear your new macintosh very soon.'

And sure enough, on the fourth day of April, the rain came at last. It rained so hard that it seemed as though it was trying to make up for the long dry days of March.

Debbie woke up and heard the rain beating on her bedroom window, and she was up and dressed in no time.

'Mummy, Mummy, it's raining at last!' she cried as she scampered downstairs. 'Can we go out now? Can I wear my lovely macintosh?'

Mother laughed. 'Well, I certainly didn't expect it to rain quite as hard as this,' she said, 'but a promise is a promise, so we will certainly go out. Help me wash and dry the dishes and make the beds, and everything else can wait till we come back.'

At last the great moment came. Debbie put on her blue flowered macintosh and hat, her shiny white boots, and a pair of blue and white plastic gloves that Mother had made her. Mother put on a pair of Wellingtons and her macintosh too, and she took her green umbrella.

'Right,' she said, 'where shall we go?'

'Up to the shops, please,' said Debbie, 'I want everyone to see my new things.'

So out into the pouring rain they went. Debbie watched with delight as it ran down the arms of her macintosh and dripped from the ends of her gloves, and giggled as it tap-tapped on top of her hat.

All the way to the shops she walked through every puddle, and at each shop she told everyone about Granny's wonderful present, and how long she'd waited for the rain.

Coming back down the hill, Debbie watched the little rivers rushing down the gutters into the drains. She watched the heavy rain coming down in thin pencils of light, making beautiful ploppity bubbles in each puddle, and stood under a big tree to feel the rain bounce even harder on her hat.

It was a wonderful day for Debbie – because of the rain!

The tall jar

Margaret Fidler

The shelf was almost covered with jars; there were large and small jam jars, small fish-paste jars, jars with pretty labels on and others with labels that Mother had written when she was bottling fruit. And, right at the back, was one very tall jar.

Mother was making some blackberry jelly, and soon there would be more jars to go on the shelf.

'Let me stick the labels on,' said Susan. She couldn't write a long word like 'blackberry' yet, but she was good at sticking things on straight.

'Thank you,' said Mother. She handed her the pile of labels, saying, 'And then perhaps you could make room on the shelf for them all.'

Susan did the sticking beautifully, but the 'making room' was a different matter. She moved some jars backwards, some forwards and some sideways, and that helped. Then Mother said that she would open a new jar of jelly for tea, so Susan chose the largest she could find, and that helped a bit more. At least she got all the new ones safely on, except one.

'Couldn't you just find space to squash the last one in?' said Mother.

Susan couldn't. Jars simply didn't squash.

So Mother looked again. 'That tall jar is empty,' she said. 'It always *is* empty. It's too tall to be of any use. We'll throw that one out.'

Susan lifted the tall jar down and the last new one took its place.

'It's rather a nice jar,' said Susan.

'It's too tall,' said Mother. 'It never has been much good. The spoons aren't long enough to reach down to the bottom. We won't miss it.'

'*I'll* miss it,' said Susan. 'May I have it?'

'But,' Mother hesitated, 'you've so much junk already in your room. I don't think you will be able to use it.'

'Oh, I know someone who'd just *love* it,' said Susan. 'It's exactly what they need.' And she ran quickly out of the room with it, before Mother could ask her any more questions.

First she went to look for Father.

'Daddy, I've got something for you. It's for storing paint brushes out in the garage,' she told him.

Daddy looked. 'It's too narrow *and* too tall. Thank you all the same,' was all he said, and then he went back to the job he was doing.

Susan tried Nicholas.

'Nicholas,' she said, 'I've got a jar for you to take when you go fishing. It's quite tall enough,' she added hopefully.

'It's a skyscraper jar,' said Nicholas. 'It's no good for fish.'

Mr Brown, next door, was cutting his lawn.

'Would you like a jar for keeping your nails and screws in?' asked Susan.

'No, thanks,' said Mr Brown. 'I use a metal box, which is much better. Anyway, I think that one's too tall.'

'Poor jar! If only you weren't made of glass I could cut a bit off you,' said Susan. So she took it up to her bedroom for the night, and found she liked it better than ever.

The next day she washed and polished the jar till it shone. Then she went to see Granny.

'Granny,' she said, 'I've a *beautiful* jar – beautifully tall and just right, if you *want* a tall jar. And she looked at it rather sadly.

'Now, that *is* a fine jar,' answered Granny, smiling. 'Are you sure Mother can spare it?'

'Oh yes, certainly she can,' said Susan. 'And it's a present from me to you. What will you do with it?'

'First,' replied Granny, 'I want to show you something very special. Fill it almost up to the top with water, please.'

Then she went to her vegetable box and fetched an onion – just an ordinary onion.

'It doesn't look much yet,' said Granny, handing it to Susan. 'But you put it on top of that tall jar. Every week when you come to see me you'll get a surprise.'

And Susan did. The first week she found that fine straight roots had grown down and reached the water.

The second week the roots were half-way down the jar, and there were five lovely green leaves, strong and sturdy, growing upwards.

The third week was even better.

'It's my favourite plant,' said Granny.

'It's the most *beautiful* onion plant,' Susan said proudly.

'It's the best I've ever grown,' went on Granny· 'But it's the jar that's done it, you know. Such a fine *tall* jar – there's plenty of room in it for the roots to stretch out. We'll be able to grow lots more onion plants in that.'

And so they did!

Wendy's week

Frances Jakeway

Wendy was nearly five, and was looking forward to going to school. She could count and write her name – and she could even manage to read a few words from her favourite book. She was also a great help with baby Andrew – Mother said she didn't know how she would manage without her. But no matter how hard Wendy tried, she could not remember the days of the week. She knew that there were seven days, and she knew their names, of course, but she could not remember the order in which they come. She would say, 'Does Tuesday come next to Friday?' or 'is Saturday after Monday?'

One day Mother said, 'Wendy, if I do one special thing every day and you help me, it will make it easier for you to remember which day it is.'

'Ooh yes,' said Wendy happily – she always liked to help Mother. 'When shall we start?'

'Let me see,' said Mother thoughtfully, 'tomorrow is Monday, and as usual I have a lot of washing to do, so we'll begin tomorrow. You can find some of your doll's clothes and I'll give you one or two things belonging to Andrew to wash as well.'

The next day was bright and sunny, so Mother began her

washing. She gave Wendy a large bowl of warm, soapy water and a few of Andrew's small vests. Wendy put on a large apron, like Mother, and began to squeeze the clothes gently in her hands. Mother's washing went swish, swish, in the machine. Soon all the clothes were rinsed and hanging in the sunshine.

The day that followed 'Washing Monday' was 'Ironing Tuesday'. Wendy found her little ironing board and toy iron, and put them beside Mother's. Together they ironed the clothes and put them neatly in a pile.

'I shall remember that ironing comes after washing,' said Wendy, 'so that means that Tuesday comes after Monday!'

'Quite right,' agreed Mother, 'you *are* learning quickly!'

On Wednesday Mother said, 'Now we have done the washing and ironing, we can polish the floor and furniture today. You can use this cloth to rub the floor where I have put on the polish.'

Baby Andrew chuckled from his pram when he saw them both on their hands and knees, rubbing away at the floor. 'I expect he wishes he could do this too,' said Wendy laughing.

It wasn't difficult for Wendy to guess the name of the next day after Wednesday, because it was the day that Mother took Andrew to the clinic to be weighed, and Wendy saw her friend John.

'It's Thursday today, isn't it Mummy?' she asked, as they were finishing breakfast.

'That's right,' said Mother. 'You can get your doll ready and then we can walk along together with our prams. John is usually at the clinic too, with his mother and baby sister.'

'Do you think they will weigh my doll as well?' asked
Wendy.

Friday was baking day, and Mother was very busy.
Wendy helped her by greasing the cake tins and sifting the
flour. She loved Friday, because making cakes was the most
special thing of all.

'Saturday comes after Friday,' said Mother, 'and Daddy
will be home. We are all going to town to buy some new curtains, and you will need some new shoes ready for school.'

'I shall call it 'Shopping Saturday!' said Wendy excitedly,
as she popped some currants into her mouth.

They had such a busy Saturday, choosing curtains and
shoes, that Wendy was quite glad when Sunday came. Sunday was quiet and peaceful, and she knew it was Sunday because she could hear the church bells ringing.

'There are only two more weeks before you go to school,'
said Mother, as she tucked Wendy into bed that night.

'Two more weeks of special days,' thought Wendy happily.

Wendy went to school on the first day of term looking
very smart in her new school clothes. She took a new clean
handkerchief every day, and printed across the corner was a
day of the week. The handkerchiefs were a present from
Mother, and, as you can guess, Wendy always chose the right
one!

Green Panes and Red

Green panes and red,
In Gran's glass door,
Make coloured pools
Along the floor.

And when there's sun,
In the dark, brown hall,
Soft rainbow lights,
Dart up the wall.

They bob and flash,
Upon each stair,
Soft green and red,
They flutter there.

Then we pretend,
My Gran and me,
That butterflies,
Have come to tea.

Kathleen Watkins

Two stories of Mr Buttons

Marion Ripley

1. Mr Buttons goes fishing

Sue, who was five years old, had two very special friends. One was Tim, the little boy who lived next door, and the other was Mr Buttons, her favourite teddy bear.

One hot summer's day, when the scent of hay was in the air and the butterflies were flitting about the lavender bush, Sue's Uncle Jim strode up the garden path, knocked on the open door, and called out, as he came into the house, 'Come on! Let's go fishing!'

Sue and Tim were looking at a picture book, but they jumped up straight away. They loved going out with Uncle Jim.

Tim had a fishing net, so he went and fetched it. Sue brought a big jam jar, and Uncle Jim tied a piece of string round the rim for a handle. Then, when Mother had given Uncle Jim some apples and chocolate to put in his pocket in case they got hungry, they set off.

Sue remembered Mr Buttons just in time, so he went along, too.

They followed a path into a valley until at last they reached a pond surrounded by trees. It was a green pond, with rushes all round the edge, and, lower down, a little silver stream was bubbling over the stones.

They all sat on the grass – Sue sat Mr Buttons on a stone – and looked into the pond. It was very still.

At first, they could only see the small, round whirligig beetles, whirling about at the top of the pond like little silver balls, and the pond skaters skating on top of the water.

Then Uncle Jim spotted a water boatman. It was like the other beetles, but it rowed itself about in the water with its long black legs, so that it looked like a tiny rowing boat with moving oars.

Next they saw another beetle, which put its tail out of the water, making a small silver bubble, and then dived to the bottom again. Uncle Jim said that it had come up for a breath of fresh air, and that they would find a lot more creatures that lived in the mud at the bottom of the pond, if they dipped the net deep down in the water.

So Tim dipped his net in and scooped up a lot of mud, and Uncle Jim showed them all the little creatures. He said that they could keep a stickleback and take it home for the pool in the garden. So Tim put it in Sue's jar, with some pond water, snails and water weed; then he washed his fishing net in the pond.

After that, Uncle Jim shared out the chocolate, and they went to look at an old nest in the trees.

Mr Buttons was still sitting on the stone. Presently, from the rushes at the end of the pond, a duck appeared. She came swimming round the edge of the pond towards him,

her tail flicking from side to side; occasionally, she would dip her head in the water and come up with a bill full of mud.

Just at that moment, a fat frog that had been sitting quietly beside Mr Buttons, suddenly jumped right over him, splash, into the pond, and swam quickly out of sight.

The duck came swimming along faster now.

'Quack, quack!' she said, as she reached the bank where Mr Buttons was sitting. 'Is this something to eat?' And she nibbled at Mr Buttons toe with her bill.

Now the stone that Mr Buttons was sitting on was rather wobbly, and when the duck began to nibble at his toe, splash! Over he went into the water, frightening the duck so much that she flapped her wings and half flew, half swam, to the other side of the pond, making such a squawking noise that Uncle Jim and Tim and Sue came running to see what had happened.

'Mr Buttons is in the water!' shouted Tim.

'Oh!' Sue cried. 'Get him out quickly!'

Uncle Jim got there first, and he picked up Tim's fishing net, plunged it into the green water and fished Mr Buttons out.

Poor Mr Buttons! He was covered in water weed, and dripping wet, but he didn't really mind because it was such fun riding in the fishing net.

Sue put Mr Buttons beside her on the grass, and Uncle Jim got out the apples, and they all ate one while Mr Buttons dried in the sun. The duck flicked her tail from side to side at the other side of the rushes, and went on scooping up mud as if the accident had nothing to do with her.

When Mr Buttons was quite dry, and they had finished their apples, they picked up the jar and the fishing net and set off for home.

'Let's carry Mr Buttons home in the fishing net,' said Sue, 'and show Daddy what we've caught.'

So they did.

Tim carried it over his shoulder all the way, and Mr Buttons enjoyed himself no end, swinging up and down in the fishing net. Daddy had the biggest surprise of his life when he saw what they had caught!

2. Mr Buttons and the snowman

It was a winter's day. The children were home from school for the Christmas holidays, and Tim had come to play with Sue.

It was bitterly cold, much too cold to play outside, but Sue and Tim didn't mind because they had new toys. Tim had brought his building set, and this kept them busy for a long time. Besides, it was baking day, and they were going to have tea round the fire, with hot buttered toast and jam, and new buns, straight out of the oven, as a special treat.

Tim finished the house he was building, and Sue made a big chair to put inside it for Mr Buttons, her teddy bear, to sit on.

Suddenly the sky grew darker, and Mother called out from the kitchen, 'It's *snowing*!'

Sue and Tim ran to the window. The white flakes dropped gently from the sky, floating down like little feathers until they covered the grass, the walls, the houses, and the pear tree. Even the little robin on the gate-post had to shake his feathers or he would have been covered too. He fluttered to the ground, made a pretty pattern with his toes, and then flew off.

It was a lovely picture, and Sue and Tim stood watching until it was time to draw the curtains and have tea.

When Father opened the door to take Tim home the snow was so deep that Sue had to lend Tim her boots, and he made a line of footprints right to the gate.

'See you tomorrow!' he called.

Next morning, Sue looked out of the bedroom window to see if Tim's footprints were still there, but they weren't; such a lot of snow had fallen in the night that it had covered them all up, and the only footprints to be seen were the milkman's. The milk was frozen in the bottles, and Mother had to thaw it out before Sue could have some on her porridge.

Presently, there was a stamping of feet outside. It was Tim, all ready for a game in the snow. He had brought back Sue's boots. Sue put them on, and soon she was ready too. Mr Buttons had to have his woolly scarf on, and then out they all went into the snow.

First they had a snowball fight to get warm, while Mr Buttons sat on the doorstep and watched them. It was such fun!

Tim caught one of Sue's snowballs, and then he rolled it in the snow until it was as big as his own head.

'Let's make a snowman, now,' said Sue.

So together they rolled the big snowball all the way to the pear tree. By then, it was bigger than Sue! In fact, it was so heavy that they couldn't push it any further, so they decided to have the snowman just there.

Next, they made another snowball and rolled *that* in the snow until it was nice and big – just a good size for the snowman's head. Their fingers were icy cold by now, so they clapped their hands to warm them. The snowman was all finished, except for his face.

'I know what we can use for his nose,' said Tim. 'A carrot!'

They both thought this was so funny that they laughed and laughed. Sue said that Mother had some carrots, and that she'd go in and fetch one.

While she was gone, Tim found some little stones for the eyes and a mouth.

Before long, Sue came running back with the carrot, and she picked Mr Buttons up from the doorstep as she came.

'Look at our lovely big snowman!' she said, and she stood Mr Buttons in the snow beside the snowman, just to show how big he was, while Tim pressed the carrot into place.

It made a beautiful nose, and they both ran indoors to tell Sue's mother about their fine snowman.

Mother was busy cooking dinner, and when she saw how cold the children's noses looked, she made them both sit down and have a bowl of steaming hot soup.

All this time Mr Buttons was standing beside the snowman.

'Br-r-r-r!' he shivered. 'How cold it is!'

'Don't you like the cold,' said the snowman softly. 'I love it. Look, it's snowing again, just as I like it. If it keeps on like this, you'll be a snowman yourself soon!'

Mr Buttons didn't like the idea at all, but he was glad that the snowman liked it because *he* would have to stay out all night by the pear tree, while Sue would come for him and he would be able to warm himself by the fire. So he chatted to the snowman as cheerfully as he could, as the snowflakes kept on falling.

Meanwhile, Mother's soup was delicious, and when Sue had finished it, Mother said she would go and look at the snowman.

Mr Buttons heard them coming – and wasn't he glad!

'Goodbye, Mr Buttons,' the snowman whispered. 'You made a fine little snowman. I shall talk to the pear tree when you are gone.'

'Goodbye, snowman!' Mr Buttons whispered back. 'I'll wave to you through the bedroom window when I go to bed tonight.'

When Sue and Tim and Mother reached the pear tree, they had such a surprise!

'Look!' shouted Tim. 'There are *two* snowmen!'

'Oh! Poor Mr Buttons!' cried Sue, picking him up and shaking the snow off him. 'You shall sit by the fire until you are nice and warm again.'

Mother helped to pat the snow off Mr Buttons. Then, after she had admired the snowman and his beautiful carrot-nose, they all went happily indoors.

Mr Buttons was soon cosy and warm again after his adventure. He had enjoyed his little talk with the snowman, for he was such a fine friendly snowman. Father thought so, too.

When Sue took Mr Buttons to bed that night, she let him look out of the bedroom window, and he waved to the snowman, just as he had promised.

Tim's birthday surprise

Kathleen Ogden

Tim was four years old. He had dark curly hair and big brown eyes. He lived with his mother and father in a flat over a sweet shop. Every Thursday afternoon Tim and his mother would leave the flat and take care of the shop while his grandmother, who owned the shop, went to visit her friends.

Tim loved Thursday afternoons. He would sit on a wooden stool behind the counter and watch everything. He could see the people gazing at the bottles of sweets in the window, and the buses, cars and bicycles hurrying past.

Many people called in the sweet shop and Mother was kept very busy serving them. Tim had never seen some of them before, but there were a few people who came every Thursday afternoon, and Tim would wait anxiously for these, who were his friends.

There was George with his cheery red face. He always came for 'six packets of mints for me and the lads'. George emptied dustbins and rode with 'the lads' on a big green refuse lorry.

Then there was old Mrs Green who walked with a stick

and who often brought Tim one of her delicious home-made cakes.

At a quarter-past four in would come Sally, the big noisy schoolgirl with long plaits. She and her friends would rush into the shop – all talking at once – trying to decide what to buy.

At about five o'clock Miss Roberts, the lady with the blue coat and quiet voice, would arrive. She usually came for chocolates, and Tim's mother explained to him that Miss Roberts was a teacher at the big new school on the other side of the town. Tim knew that he would soon be five and that then he, too, would be able to go to school.

But Tim did not really want to go to school. He liked being with Mother. He liked fetching the paper bags from underneath the counter and helping to keep the shop tidy. He did, however, have one special wish. He wanted to serve the customers. Mother explained that only grown-ups could serve in shops and that, in any case, before Tim could do this he must go to school and learn to read, to write and to use money.

One Thursday, the week before Tim's fifth birthday, Miss Roberts came into the shop as usual. Mother sent Tim to stand by the door to look for Father while she and Miss Roberts talked quietly together. Tim thought this most strange, but he did as he was told. 'Goodbye, I'll see you next week,' said Miss Roberts to Tim and his mother as she left the shop.

The week passed quickly, and once again it was Thursday, the day for minding the shop. But – most important of all –

it was Tim's birthday. Mother and Father said 'Happy birthday, Tim,' when he sat down to breakfast. By the side of Tim's plate were four envelopes and one tiny parcel. The envelopes contained brightly coloured cards – one from Mother and Father, one from Grandmother and the other two from an auntie and uncle – and inside the parcel was a small yellow van. Although the van was exactly what Tim wanted, he felt rather disappointed and wondered whether it was his only birthday present.

As Father left for work, he said, 'Have a happy day, Tim. I shall be home early for tea, as I expect you will have lots of things to tell me.'

The morning passed quickly. After lunch Mother said, 'Come along, Tim, we must get ready or we shall be late.'

'But Mummy,' said Tim, 'it's Thursday afternoon and we always look after the shop.'

'Yes, but we're not today, Tim. Now hurry along.'

Soon Tim and his mother were on a large red bus speeding towards the outskirts of the town. When it stopped, Mother said, 'Come on, Tim,' and they both stepped off the bus.

They went through some enormous gates and along a path which led to a smooth glass door. Tim felt very strange. What was Mother doing bringing him to this place on his birthday? Mother held his hand firmly, and they went inside the building. Everywhere looked so big. In front of them was a long corridor with lots of doors. Tim felt rather frightened. A tall lady with grey hair came forward. She smiled. 'Ah, Mrs Jones and Tim,' she said. 'Please come this way.'

'Well, Tim,' she continued, 'my name is Miss Graham. I

am the headmistress of this school and I look after all the girls and boys. Miss Roberts told me that it was your birthday, so I thought that your mother might like to bring you along to school today as a special treat.'

While Miss Graham talked, they walked along the corridor until they reached a door painted bright red with a number five and a picture of a teddy bear on it.

'Here we are,' she said. 'This is Miss Roberts' room.' She knocked on the door and they all walked in.

The room was gay with brightly coloured pictures on the walls. There were many tables and chairs and lots of children. Some were building with bricks; others were painting . . . and then Tim saw it! In the far corner of the room was a sweet shop, with scales on the counter and jars of colourful sweets on the shelves. Tim let go of Mother's hand and walked over to the shop. A little boy stood behind the counter. He had fair hair and a smiling face.

'Hello,' he said, 'my name is John. Do you want to play?' Tim discovered that the sweets and money were not real, but otherwise it looked almost like Grandmother's shop. He started to play. He weighed sweets, put them in paper bags and gave them to the children who came from a little house on the other side of the room. Tim had almost forgotten about Mother, when she suddenly appeared before him. 'Well,' she laughed, 'you have enjoyed yourself. But come along now. We must get home in good time for tea.'

'Thank you very much,' said Tim to Miss Roberts, Miss Graham and the children.

On the bus Tim looked up at his mother and said,

'Mummy, I think I should like to go to school now that I am five.'

When they arrived home, Grandmother and Father were waiting. The table was laid for tea, and in the middle was a beautiful birthday cake with five blue candles, all lit. After tea, while Tim was telling his father all about his adventures at school, his mother quietly lifted a brown box from underneath the sideboard and handed it to him.

'The yellow car was only part of your present, Tim,' she said, smiling. 'Happy birthday again.'

Inside the box was a real leather satchel, a grey suit and a cap with a red and white badge on it.

'Oh,' said Tim, 'what a lovely birthday present. Please, when can I go to school?'

'Next Monday,' Mother told him.

Soon Tim was tucked up in bed, and just before he fell asleep he thought to himself, 'I'm sure school is a lovely place, but the thing I liked best was serving in the shop.'

Old Witch

Somebody says an old bent witch,
Lives in the cottage down Broomstick Lane,
Dressed in a cloak as black as pitch,
Somebody peeped through the window pane,

Somebody saw her stirring a pot,
Of feathers and bones and fur and brain,
Fox gloves and hemlock bubbling hot,
Somebody saw her plain as plain.

Somebody saw her mixing spells,
On a stormy night of wind and rain,
Of cobwebs, nettles and dried harebells,
Somebody peeped through the window pane.

It wasn't me. I think it was Jane.

Kathleen Watkins

Sally learns to cook

Elspeth Ricks

It was a very wet Saturday morning! Down came the rain splashing on the garden path, and Sally felt very disappointed. Mother and Father had given her a lovely blue and yellow scooter for her birthday, and she so much wanted to play with it in the garden. 'Bother the rain,' she said. 'It's spoilt all my fun!'

'It *is* disappointing,' said Mother, 'but I know of something nice you can do instead. Granny is coming for tea, and you can help me make the scones. Soon you will be able to make them all by yourself!'

So they washed their hands, and Mother lit the oven and turned it up to 'Hot'. 'Now,' she said, 'we must get out the flour, butter and milk. You can sieve the flour into the cooking bowl for me and add a pinch of salt, and I'll rub in some butter until it looks just like breadcrumbs. Then I'll add a little milk and mix it in with the wooden spoon until we have a nice soft dough. Next we must sprinkle the baking board and rolling pin with flour, and you can roll the dough gently until it is smooth and about as thick as the pastry cutter. We'll cut the dough into circles with a fluted cutter to make the scones look pretty, and brush the top of each one with the pastry brush dipped in milk, to make them nice and shiny. Then we can put them on the baking tin and into the hot oven.'

When the scones were in the oven, Mother said, 'Now we can leave them until the kitchen clock says 12 o'clock. We can wash up the cooking things and put them tidily away while the scones are cooking.'

Mother put out a wire tray on which to cool the scones, and by then it was time to open the oven door. Mother opened it gently, and there were the scones, twelve of them, risen to twice their size and golden brown and shiny!

'They are very nicely cooked,' said Mother. 'Sally, watch carefully how I take the baking tin out of the oven with my thick oven gloves so that I don't burn myself!'

'Now I'll show you how to whip up some cream, so that we can have scones with jam and whipped cream for tea! Next week you can make the scones yourself, but I will be there in case you need any help!'

Sally set the table with the best pale green tea-set, and Mother had made a sponge cake because it was Granny's favourite. She also made some dainty little sandwiches, and decorated the plate with sprigs of parsley.

It was a very enjoyable tea party, and Granny was very interested to hear how Sally had helped to make the scones.

Before Granny went home she said to Sally, 'I believe you are going to be a good cook like your mother, and when I get home I shall look out the cooking things she had when she was a little girl. There is a pastry board, a rolling pin, a flour bin and a cooking bowl, all sorts of little cake and pie tins, and even a small egg whisk. You will be coming to see me next weekend and I shall have them all ready for you to take home!'

'It *has* been a good day, after all,' said Sally, 'even though it did rain!'

Nicholas and Mr Frog

Margaret Fidler

Mr Frog just arrived—no one ever knew how. One day in the spring, Nicholas went into the garden to see his friends the fish, and there he was in the pond. He was sitting on a thick stem of a water lily, with the top of his head just above the water.

Nicholas *was* surprised to see Mr Frog.

And Mr Frog was surprised to see Nicholas. He spread out his long legs and dived right down to the mud and dead leaves at the bottom.

But, as time went by, he became quite tame and would sit basking in the sun, even when Nicholas and Susan, his sister, were there watching him. The fish seemed to like his company, too, and would swim round him in a circle; sometimes, if it was too hot, they would even get close enough to nudge him up a bit on his stem, so that they could enjoy the shade of the large lily leaves.

As the summer went on, Mr Frog grew bigger and fatter, but the pond grew muddier and greener, so that the bottom could hardly be seen at all, even after a shower of rain.

'The pond is very dirty,' said Father. 'I must get the fish

out and give it a good clean. They don't like it all slimy and green—and it looks so untidy.'

'But what about Mr Frog?' asked Nicholas. 'He needs to have the mud and the dead leaves for his home.'

So Father said they would take Mr Frog out, put him in a bucket and take him to the river's edge, where he would soon settle down and make a new home.

Susan started to cry. 'He will be lonely without us and the fish,' she said. 'We're his friends.'

Nicholas cried. 'There are ducks on the river,' he said. 'Ducks eat frogs.'

At the thought of Mr Frog being eaten, they both cried louder than ever. 'Why can't we just put the mud back again?' they asked. But Father said that that wasn't the idea of cleaning out the pond—after all, it was a fish pond, and fish needed fairly clear water to keep them well and happy.

The children went to see Granny, who was a great admirer of Mr Frog.

Granny said that no frog would be happy in a pond which hadn't a place at the bottom for him to hide away in when the sun got too hot or too bright. 'But Daddy's right, too,' she said. 'If the water gets very dirty, it could make the fish ill. So let me think now.'

Granny thought hard, and Nicholas and Susan kept very quiet, hoping that once again Granny would come to the rescue with one of those splendid ideas she often had.

At last she went out to her garden shed. When she came back she was carrying a large flower pot which she had been meaning to throw away because one side was broken quite badly.

She stood the broken pot upside down on the table. 'This would make a fine, shady frog-house,' she said. 'The piece that has broken out can be a door for Mr Frog to go in and out. We'll put it upside down like this on the bottom of the pond, with a large stone on top so that it can't fall over. Then we'll tuck in a few dead leaves and some moss and a smooth stone or two, just the way he likes it. You'll see—he will be very happy to stay in the pond, however clean Daddy makes it.'

And Mr Frog *was* happy. He soon settled into his new home, and he liked it very much. Sometimes the fish went inside to visit him, but they did not stay long because, after all, it was a frog home.

Then, one morning when Nicholas went to the pond, he had a big surprise. There was Mr Frog as usual, sunning himself on the stone above his house—but he seemed to have shrunk!

'Come and look at Mr Frog,' he called to Mother. 'He's suddenly got smaller.'

Mother came to look, and she laughed. 'That's not Mr Frog,' she said, 'it's a new frog who's come to share the lovely new home with him.'

Granny was delighted. 'Well, well,' she said, 'so now there's a Mrs Frog, too! How very nice!'

And so it was, wasn't it?

Simon and the dandelion clocks

Elizabeth MacDonald

'Oh, thank you! They're lovely!' said Simon's mother, when his father brought home a bunch of flowers for her. She put them in a vase of water and stood it on a table in the living-room. She gave the flowers fresh water every day, and as each one started to droop and fade, she threw it away and re-arranged the ones that were left. When there were no flowers left at all, she washed the vase and put it away.

'I wish I could get Mummy some more flowers,' thought Simon, but although he had some money in his money-box, he was too young to go to the flower shop on his own, and he wanted the flowers to be a surprise.

He gazed through the window at the flower beds in front of the block of flats where they lived. But the flowers growing there were for the people to look at. No one was allowed to pick them.

He was still looking at them, and thinking how pretty they were, when he saw his granny coming up the path. He had forgotten it was Friday. Granny usually came to see them on Fridays, and if it was a fine afternoon she would take Simon for a walk while his mother made some cakes for tea.

'Granny's here!' he called to his mother, and he ran to meet her, forgetting all about the flowers.

That afternoon Simon's granny took him to the park near by. There was a children's playground in one corner, and Simon went on the swings and the roundabout, and sat on the big, red horse, holding on tight while Granny pushed it backwards and forwards.

Then they walked across the grass to see if there were any fish in the little stream on the far side of the park. They couldn't see any, but Simon dropped a twig into the water and watched it float out of sight. Suddenly he noticed some patches of bright yellow among the clumps of grass farther along the stream, and when he ran to have a closer look he saw that they were flowers.

'Aren't they pretty, Granny?' he said, stroking the yellow, feathery petals with his fingers. 'Do they belong to anyone?'

'They belong to everyone. They're wild flowers,' said Granny. 'They are called dandelions. Would you like to pick some?'

'Yes, please,' said Simon. 'I want to give some to Mummy.'

He picked some of the dandelions and carried them home carefully. His mother was very pleased, and she put them in a vase of water on the table in the living-room, just as she had done with his father's flowers. She gave them fresh water every day, but by the following Friday, when Simon's granny came again, they had all drooped, so she had to throw them away.

Granny took Simon to the park again, and before they went home they went along to pick some more dandelions. But there were only enough for a small bunch, because where the yellow flowers had been before, there were now fluffy white balls on the stalks instead.

'Look! The dandelions have turned into clocks!' said Granny.

'Clocks?' said Simon, looking puzzled.

'We called them dandelion clocks when I was a little girl,' said Granny. 'We used to blow on them and count: One o'clock . . . two o'clock . . . three o'clock . . . and so on, until all the fluff had floated away, taking the seeds with it.' And she showed him how the fluffy white balls were made up of lots of little white parachutes, each with a brown seed on the end.

Simon picked the dandelion clocks, and as he blew on them the seeds floated away on their tiny parachutes; then the breeze caught them and carried them a little way before dropping them to the ground.

Puff! '. . . One o'clock . . .' Puff! '. . . Two o'clock . . .' Puff! '. . . Three o'clock . . .' chanted Simon. Once he had to count up to ten o'clock before all the fluff had gone.

'The seeds will grow into dandelion plants, and the plants will have flowers,' said Granny.

'And the flowers will turn into more dandelion clocks with more seeds,' said Simon.

There was only one fluffy white ball left. 'One o'clock . . . two o'clock . . . three o'clock . . . four o'clock . . . five o'clock!' counted Simon, after each puff. 'Five o'clock? It's time for tea, Granny!' he laughed, and picking up the small bunch of dandelions that he had gathered, he skipped across the grass beside his granny as they made their way home.

The Window Cleaner

With cloth and pail comes Mr Green,
To rub the window panes,
On stormy days he's rarely seen,
It's useless when it rains.
On fine days if he comes to clean
The windows during tea,
Then I smile out at Mr Green,
And he smiles in at me.

Kathleen Watkins